Here is the big-thinking Which Way crew who will guide you through Alaska:

Eagle-Eye Ellie is the Which Way driver. She looks forward to seeing her old friend, bush pilot Ava Aeter.

Ralph is eager to join the fun at the World Eskimo and Indian Olympics.

Table of Contents

WHO is heading for the WHICH WAY HALL OF FAME?

WHAT will be in the WHICH WAY MUSEUM?

WHERE will the WHICH WAY SUPERMAX MOVIE be filmed?

WHALE, WHALE!

The Which Way team begins their adventure at sea. The crew members board a ship to cruise through the Inside Passage of southeast Alaska. As Ellie scans the water for whales, Mr. Memory spouts off facts about Alaska's wildlife: "Did you know that Alaska has more bald eagles than the rest of the United States put together? Did you know that black bears are often brown? Did you know there are whales in the water all around us?"

Mr. Memory is so busy talking that he misses seeing two whales right by the boat! You need to be ready at all times in a state famous for its wildlife. See if you can find a place in the grid on page 3 for the fourteen Alaska animals listed below. Fit only the words in capital letters. Then see what is waiting at the bottom of the page.

4 letters
Arctic **TERN**

5 letters
MOOSE
POLAR bear
Dall **SHEEP**
Killer **WHALE**

6 letters
KODIAK bear
MUSK OX
PUFFIN
SALMON

7 letters
CARIBOU
GRIZZLY bear
SEA LION

9 letters
CORMORANT
PTARMIGAN

Have you found a place for all the animal names? Some of the boxes are shaded. Write the letters from those boxes here:

__ __ __ __ __ __ __ __ __

Now unscramble those letters to spell the name of a famous Alaskan on page 28:

__ __ __ __ __ __ __ __ __

You can cross off this person.

3

Face Facts

The ship slides into a slip in Ketchikan for the night. This small city is sometimes called the "Gateway to Alaska." It is the first city reached when traveling north from the continental U.S.

Ketchikan is a center for native Tlingit (pronounced "Clinkit") people. The Tlingit are known for their totem-carving skills. Ketchikan has more totems than anywhere else in the world.

At Totem Bight State Park the next morning, Jack sees faces staring at him from all directions. The faces on totem poles often tell a story about how animals affected a family's life. These totems have a story to tell you, too. Solve the picture code and then face the bottom of page 5.

Have you solved the totem code? Now turn to page 28. Use the clue to cross off one famous Alaskan.

On Ice

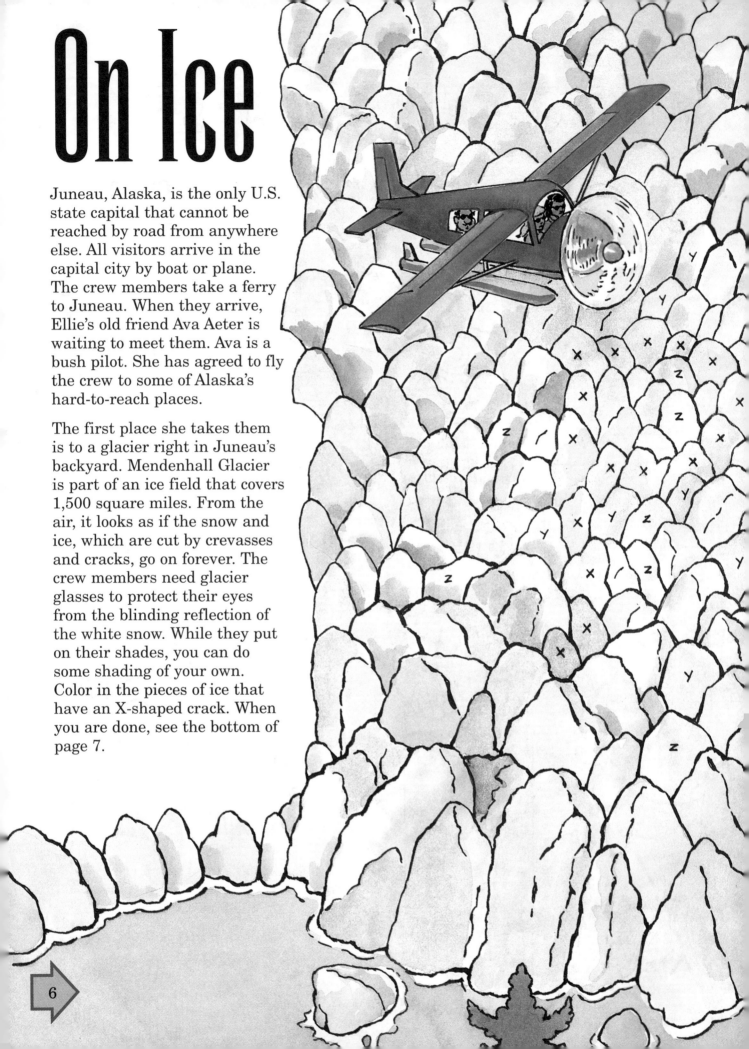

Juneau, Alaska, is the only U.S. state capital that cannot be reached by road from anywhere else. All visitors arrive in the capital city by boat or plane. The crew members take a ferry to Juneau. When they arrive, Ellie's old friend Ava Aeter is waiting to meet them. Ava is a bush pilot. She has agreed to fly the crew to some of Alaska's hard-to-reach places.

The first place she takes them is to a glacier right in Juneau's backyard. Mendenhall Glacier is part of an ice field that covers 1,500 square miles. From the air, it looks as if the snow and ice, which are cut by crevasses and cracks, go on forever. The crew members need glacier glasses to protect their eyes from the blinding reflection of the white snow. While they put on their shades, you can do some shading of your own. Color in the pieces of ice that have an X-shaped crack. When you are done, see the bottom of page 7.

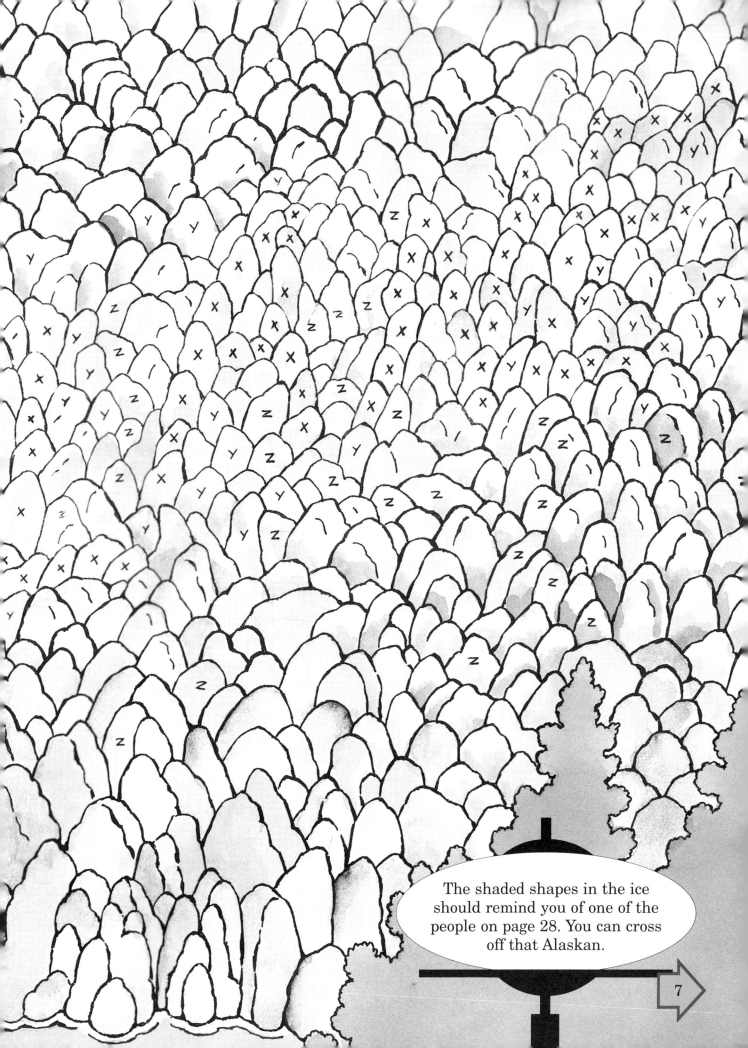

The shaded shapes in the ice
should remind you of one of the
people on page 28. You can cross
off that Alaskan.

Fancy Footwork

The crew is ready and eager to see more of Alaska. Ava turns her plane southwest and flies to Sitka. This city was established about 200 years ago by a Russian named Alexander Baranof. Sitka was the center of Russian Alaska until the United States purchased the territory in 1867.

Ralph and Mr. Memory go for a walk and discover the New Archangel Dancers, a group of Russian folk dancers, performing in downtown Sitka. While they watch the footwork, you can do some legwork to find the next clue. Circle the letter of each correct answer. Then shuffle over to the bottom of page 9.

Don't Forget Your Map!
Your map of Alaska has all the information you need to answer these questions.

1. Which of these is *not* a major lake on your Alaska map?

    a. Naknek   **e. Becharof**
          i. Kuskokwim

2. Yup'ik Eskimos love *akutak*. What is it?

  b. a musical instrument like a mandolin
    c. a traditional board game
      d. a kind of ice cream

3. What is Alaska's state land animal?

    i. moose   **o. grizzly bear**
        u. Arctic fox

4. In what year did Mt. Katmai erupt?

   s. 1897   **t. 1912**   **r. 1917**

7. About how many streams in Alaska are named Bear Creek?

   e. 7   **n. 17**   **o. 70**

5. Which of these places is the busiest seaplane port in the world?

   a. Lake Hood   **g. Kodiak**
   h. Glacier Bay

8. How far is Barrow from the North Pole?

   d. 800 miles   **l. 500 miles**
   s. 300 miles

6. Which of these three cities is smaller than Juneau?

   p. Fairbanks   **r. Ketchikan**
   m. Anchorage

Have you answered all of the questions? Write the letters that you circled, in order, in the spaces below to complete a clue.

Eliminate the person associated with the

__ __ __ __ __ __ __ __ .

Now turn to page 28 and cross one more Alaskan off your list.

Green Giants

Ava flies the crew up the Alaska coast to Anchorage. Nearly half of all Alaskans live in the state's largest city. The crew decides to split up to explore the area. Ava, Ellie, and Jack hurry off to the Matanuska Valley, near Anchorage. This region has Alaska's best farming soil. Because of the long summer days, crops here grow and grow and grow. Many record-breaking vegetables come from here.

The crew members arrive in time for a produce competition. They marvel at the big veggies the prizewinners have grown. Ava, Jack, and Ellie guess how much could be made from each vegetable. Use the facts below to figure out whose guesses are correct. Then check the bottom of page 11.

> I bet that would make 60 loaves of zucchini bread.

26 POUNDS

FACT BOX

- One pumpkin pie uses 4 pounds of pumpkin.
- Two loaves of zucchini bread use 1 pound of zucchini.
- Three servings of coleslaw use 1 pound of cabbage.

75 POUNDS

PIPING HOT

Mr. Memory takes Ralph and WEB.STER on a trip to Valdez, east of Anchorage. This is where the Trans-Alaska Pipeline ends. Oil was discovered at Prudhoe Bay in 1968. From 1974 to 1977, crews worked to build an 800-mile-long pipeline to bring the oil across land to Valdez. From here, it is sent out on tanker ships.

The pipeline is raised above the ground so that it doesn't disturb migrating animals, and so that the hot oil does not melt the always-frozen soil. It is built in a zigzag pattern so that it won't crack if there's an earthquake. You'll need to zig and zag between your map and this page to answer all the questions. When you finish, use the code letters to complete the message at the top of page 13. Then ooze down to the bottom of the page.

1. What large city is due north of Seward?

___ ___ ___ ___ ___ ___ ___ ___ ___
  1   2   3

2. What ship spilled its load of oil in Prince William Sound in 1989?

___ ___ ___ ___ ___   ___ ___ ___ ___ ___ ___
        4   5

3. Who was the first woman to reach the top of Mt. McKinley?

___ ___ ___ ___ ___ ___ ___   ___ ___ ___ ___ ___ ___ ___ ___ ___
  6   7   8

4. What chain of islands stretches west of Alaska?

___ ___ ___ ___ ___ ___ ___ ___
  9 10   11

5. What is Alaska's state fish?

___ ___ ___ ___ ___   ___ ___ ___ ___ ___ ___ ___
  12   13   14

Highlights
WHICH WAY
USA?

STATE MAP

Don't Forget Your Map!
You can find all the answers to these questions on your map of Alaska.

12

MESSAGE
Cross off

$\overline{}$ $\overline{}$ $\overline{}$ $\overline{}$ $\overline{}$ $\overline{}$ $\quad$ $\overline{}$ $\overline{}$ $\overline{}$ $\overline{}$ $\overline{}$ $\quad$ $\overline{}$ $\overline{}$ $\overline{}$ $\overline{}$
1 9 9 11 2 10 7 4 8 5 13 11 2 1 11

$\overline{}$ $\overline{}$ $\overline{}$ $\overline{}$ $\overline{}$ $\quad$ $\overline{}$ $\overline{}$ $\overline{}$ $\overline{}$ $\quad$ $\overline{}$ $\quad$ $\overline{}$ $\overline{}$ $\overline{}$ $\quad$ $\overline{}$.
6 10 3 12 14 7 12 11 2 13 1 14 5 11

Turn to the Word Box on
page 29 and write this
clue on the line.

13

Mush!

Meanwhile, Jack, Ava, and Ellie travel to the town of Knik, north of Anchorage. They head straight to the Mushers Hall of Fame. Here, they learn about many Alaskan sled-dog races. The most famous one is the 1,100-mile-long Iditarod, which runs from Anchorage to Nome. The Iditarod follows parts of two trails that used to be sled-dog mail routes. The race has been held every March since 1973.

At the museum, the crew members meet a musher, who brings them to a farm where her sled dogs are raised. She explains that the dogs don't always stay in their own houses. In fact, only the alpha, or lead, dog sleeps in its own house. She calls all of the dogs to come greet the crew members. Follow the tracks of the dogs to figure out which dog came from the doghouse that matches its collar. That is the alpha dog that will lead you to a clue at the bottom of page 15.

14

Did you figure out which one is the alpha dog? Look at the number on that dog's collar. Use it to complete this clue for page 29:

Cross off all the words with _____ letters.

Truly Spectacular

The group regroups in Anchorage and boards Ava's plane for a flight to see Mt. McKinley, North America's highest peak. Because so much of Alaska is remote and the distances are so great, many people use airplanes just like cars. In Alaska, taking a tour from the air is called "flightseeing."

On the plane, Mr. Memory starts feeling queasy looking out the windows. He decides to keep his eyes inside by reading Ava's logbook. Tourists who have flown with her have written their thoughts about their Alaska trips. Mr. M. realizes that several of them have their facts confused. Read each entry and decide whether or not it is true. Then fly over to the bottom of page 17.

Don't Forget Your Map!
The *back* of your map of Alaska contains all the facts you need to solve this puzzle.

We saw the Iditarod. We caught all the action from stop #36 where the mushers and dogs rested on their way to Nome. What a thrill!

We stopped in Valdez near the Trans-Alaska Pipeline. Can you believe the oil we saw coming out had begun its trip through the pipeline more than five days earlier?

Mount McKinley is spectacular. I never realized that it was the same mountain as Denali, but it is. That is the old Russian name for the peak.

We saw a Native American carving a totem pole in Sitka. Imagine! Totems are still carved from cedar trees as they were long ago.

I saw a moose in Anchorage. Ava told me not to be so surprised. About 1,000 of them live within the city limits.

I loved Kotzebue and its friendly people. The Tlingit have lived there for centuries.

Have you figured out which entries are true?
Use that information to find the clue for page 29.

If half are true,
cross off the words with only four letters.

If more than half are true,
cross off the words with five letters.

If fewer than half are true,
cross off the words with a K in them.

Gold-Medal Clue

Ava drops off the gang in Fairbanks. The World Eskimo and Indian Olympics are taking place here. All of the competitions are based on local Native American traditions. Blanket tossing, for instance, was how the natives spotted wild game animals. Other events include the four-man carry, high kick, ear pull, and greased-pole walk. These unusual games develop mental and physical skills that have helped people survive in the rugged Alaska countryside.

While Ralph tries out the blanket toss, some of the medal winners are talking to the Which Way crew. Use the facts given on page 19 to figure out which one of the competitors has a clue for you. Then jump to the bottom of that page when you're done.

FACTS

The person with the clue
- is not wearing a white shirt;
- won a silver medal;
- is a woman;
- is not wearing gloves.

Did you figure out which person has the clue for you? Look on his or her shirt for a letter. Use it to complete this clue for page 29:

Cross off words that begin with the letter ____.

See the Lights

Ellie gets behind the wheel again and drives north and east out of Fairbanks. As darkness falls, the crew is thrilled to see shimmering, colorful lights in the northern sky. WEB.STER informs them that they are looking at the aurora borealis. The glowing light is made of charged particles that are energized by the sun. This beautiful sight is also called northern lights because the farther north you go, the more likely you are to see it.

While the crew members are filling their eyes with northern lights, you can fill in the grid on page 21 with Alaska sites. When you have written in all of the names, gaze at the box at the bottom of the page.

ACROSS

3. _____ Peninsula (home of Nome)
4. Southeastern city south of Glacier Bay National Park and Preserve
6. Island and city known for bears, south of Katmai National Park
8. Highway that runs next to the Trans-Alaska Pipeline
10. ____ ____ Sound (body of water south of Valdez)

DOWN

1. Large city on the Tanana River near the town of North Pole
2. Sea or strait off Alaska's west coast
5. Town just south of Skagway
7. _____ Fjords National Park (area south of Anchorage)
8. Alaska's capital city
9. Highest mountain in Denali National Park

WHICH WAY USA?

STATE MAP

Don't Forget Your Map!
Your map of Alaska has all the information you need to fill in the crossword.

Have you filled in the crossword? Some of the boxes are shaded. Write the letters from those boxes, in order from top to bottom and left to right, in the spaces below to complete a clue.

On page 30, you can cross off the site located in

___ ___ ___ ___ ___ ___ .

Circular Thinking

The crew continues toward the towns of Circle and Circle Hot Springs. The road leading northeast out of Fairbanks ends at these towns near the Yukon River. Both Circle and Circle Hot Springs are near the Arctic Circle. They are so far north that on the longest day of the year the sun does not set here. Ellie and Ralph decide to relax with a dip at the resort in Circle Hot Springs.

You can relax by dipping into a word puzzle. Each clue around the circle defines a three-letter word that is different from the words before and after it by just one letter. (For example, ICE, ACE, and ACT differ from each other by just one letter.) Fill in all of the words, then circle down to the bottom of the page.

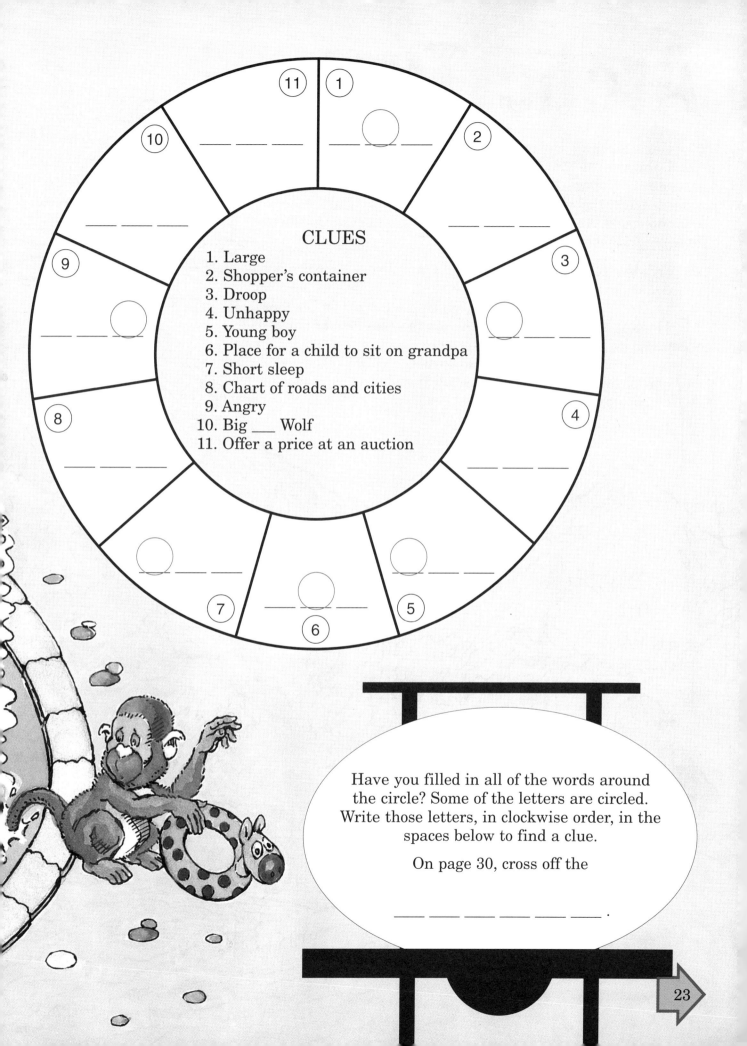

CLUES

1. Large
2. Shopper's container
3. Droop
4. Unhappy
5. Young boy
6. Place for a child to sit on grandpa
7. Short sleep
8. Chart of roads and cities
9. Angry
10. Big ___ Wolf
11. Offer a price at an auction

Have you filled in all of the words around the circle? Some of the letters are circled. Write those letters, in clockwise order, in the spaces below to find a clue.

On page 30, cross off the

___ ___ ___ ___ ___ ___ ___ .

Arctic Turns

The next morning, the crew boards Ava's plane for a flight north toward the top of the continent. At noon, the plane lands in Gates of the Arctic National Park and Preserve. In this remote park, there are no maintained roads or trails, no telephones, shelters, park rangers, or first-aid stations. Just how big Alaska is starts to sink in!

Jack leads a hike up a nearby peak. On the way, he points out some of the native animal and plant life, including ptarmigan, beaver, and forget-me-nots. After getting a blister on his foot, Mr. Memory finds himself wishing for the comforts of home. He wishes so hard that he starts seeing things in the scenery. Find the hidden tea kettle, slipper, radio, pillow, coffee mug, and toothbrush. When you have found all the objects, find the box on the bottom of page 25.

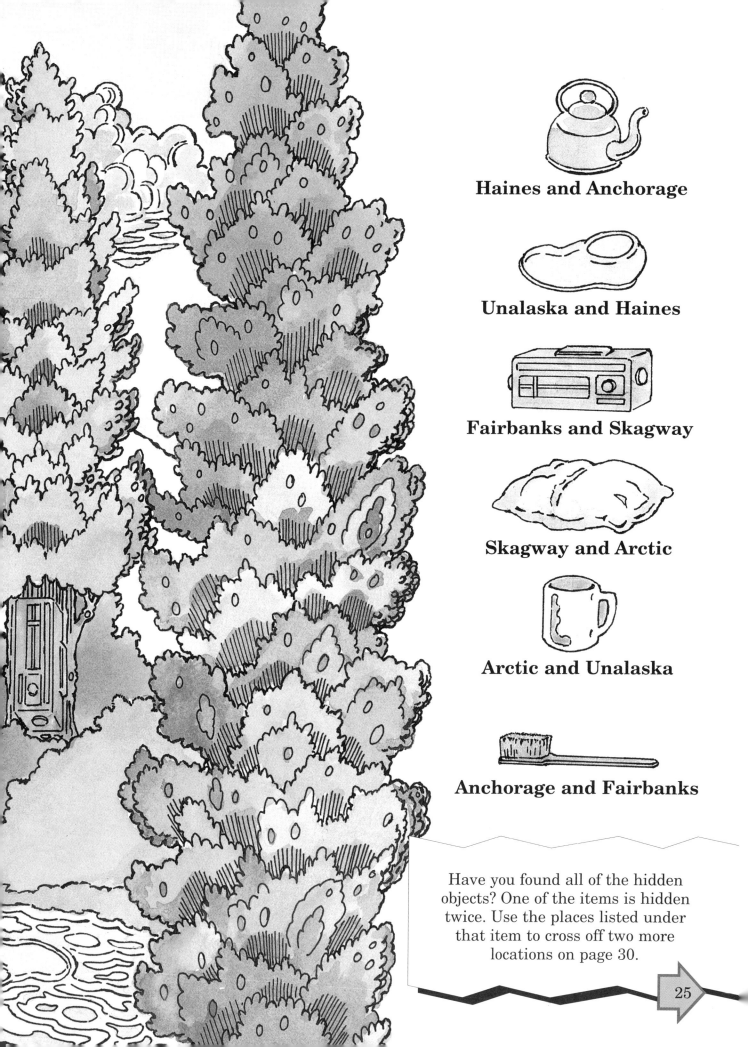

Haines and Anchorage

Unalaska and Haines

Fairbanks and Skagway

Skagway and Arctic

Arctic and Unalaska

Anchorage and Fairbanks

Have you found all of the hidden objects? One of the items is hidden twice. Use the places listed under that item to cross off two more locations on page 30.

SNOW BALL

Back on the plane, Ava flies the crew to Barrow. This is the northernmost town in the entire United States. In the summer, the sun doesn't set in Barrow for eighty-four days. Of course, it is dark all day long in the winter for eighty-four days as well!

More than 60 percent of the people in this frozen outpost have Inuit roots. They live with white flakes so much of the year that they use specific words to describe different types of snow. In fact, no one seems to know how many of these words there are.

Mr. Memory sorted out nineteen words for snow. Find them in the grid on page 27 to pack off with the last clue. Look forward, backward, up, down, and diagonally. When you've found them all, make tracks to the bottom of the page.

WORDS FOR SNOW

AKELRORAK (newly drifting snow)

ANIUK (snow for melting into water)

ANIUVAK (snowbank)

APINGAUT (first snowfall)

APUN (snow)

AUKSALAK (melting snow)

AYAK (snow on clothes)

KATIKSUNIK (light snow)

KIKSRUKAK (glazed snow in a thaw)

MASSAK (snow and water)

MAVSA (snowdrift overhead)

MITAILAK (soft snow over an ice floe)

NATIGVIK (snowdrift)

NUTAGAK (powder snow)

PERKSERTOK (drifting snow)

POKAKTOK (salt-like snow)

PUKAK (sugar snow)

SILLIK (hard, crusty snow)

SISUUK (avalanche)

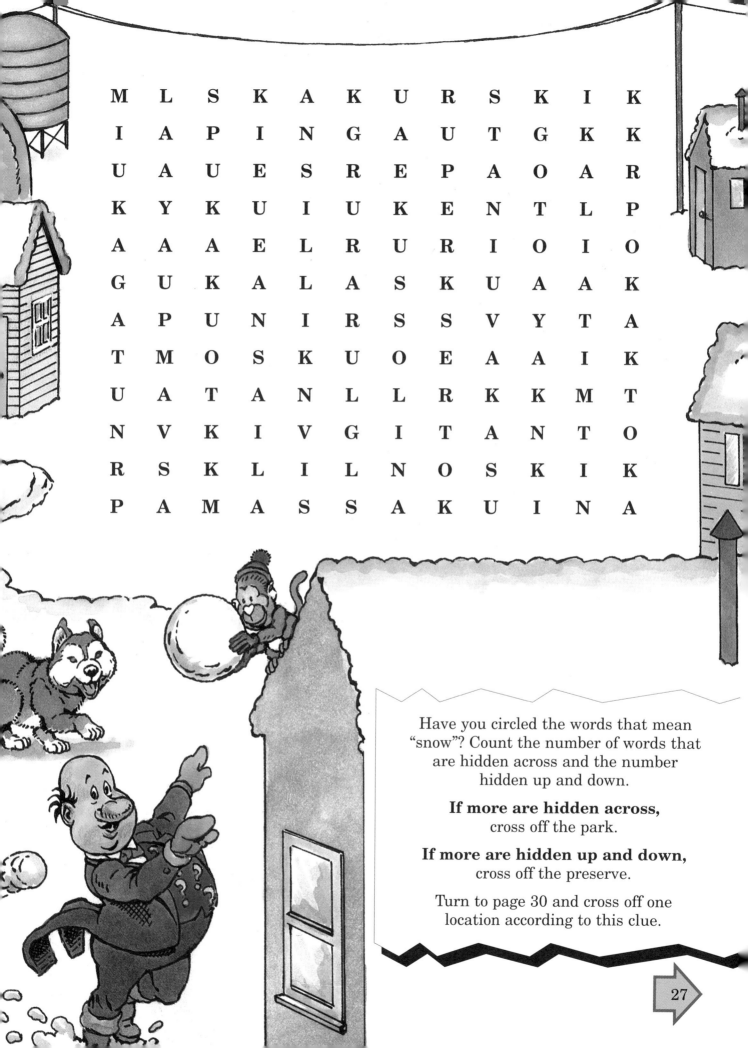

M L S K A K U R S K I K
I A P I N G A U T G K K
U A U E S R E P A O A R
K Y K U I U K E N T L P
A A A E L R U R I O I O
G U K A L A S K U A A K
A P U N I R S S V Y T A
T M O S K U O E A A I K
U A T A N L L R K K M T
N V K I V G I T A N T O
R S K L I L N O S K I K
P A M A S S A K U I N A

Have you circled the words that mean "snow"? Count the number of words that are hidden across and the number hidden up and down.

If more are hidden across, cross off the park.

If more are hidden up and down, cross off the preserve.

Turn to page 30 and cross off one location according to this clue.

Who?

Which famous Alaskan will enter the Which Way Hall of Fame? To find out, you need to solve the puzzles on pages 2 through 11. Each puzzle will help you cross one person off the list. When there is only one person left, he or she is the hall-of-famer!

Susan Butcher
Four-time winner of the Anchorage-to-Nome Iditarod Trail Sled Dog Race

Carl Ben Eielson
Pioneering bush pilot who made many flights over Alaska in the 1920s

Jack London
Author of Alaska-based adventure stories, including *The Call of the Wild*

Joseph Juneau
Gold miner and prospector who sparked the Alaska Gold Rush

Howard Rock
Alaskan Native American painter and scrimshaw (whalebone-carving) artist

Edward Lewis Bartlett
Politician who helped Alaska gain statehood and served as one of its first senators

The person going into the Hall of Fame is:

What?

One thing from Alaska has been chosen to be displayed in the Which Way Museum. To find out what it is, you'll need to solve the puzzles on pages 12 through 19. Each puzzle will give you a clue to write below.

Pages 12-13: Cross off _____.

Pages 14-15: Cross off all the words with _____ letters.

Pages 16-17: Cross off all the words with _____.

Pages 18-19: Cross off all the words that begin with the letter _____.

Use these clues to cross out words in this Word Box.

WORD BOX

A TOTEM BEAR KAYAK SLED

CABIN WALRUS WHICH FLOWER

WAS CARIBOU THE SNOWSHOE

INVENTED MANY TRAIN BY ALASKAN

SCRIMSHAW DOGS COLD NATIVES

Now that you have solved all the puzzles and crossed off all the extra words, write the remaining words below to spell out the answer.

The item that will go into the Which Way Museum is:

_____ _____ , _____ _____

_____ _____ _____ .

Where?

One Alaskan location has been chosen to be featured in the Which Way Supermax Movie. To find out where the filming will be, solve the puzzles on pages 20 through 27. Each puzzle will help you cross off one or more of the famous places below. When you have solved all the puzzles, the one place that is left is your answer.

Earthquake Park
Anchorage site where 130 acres of land were leveled by the 1964 earthquake

Unalaska
Second-largest island in the Aleutian Islands chain

Chilkat Bald Eagle Preserve
Site north of Haines where more than 3,500 bald eagles gather in the late fall

University of Alaska Museum
Museum in Fairbanks filled with objects of cultural and scientific interest

Klondike Gold Rush Park
Skagway's monument to the miners who came looking for gold in the late 1800s

Gates of the Arctic National Park
National park in the Brooks Range of remote north-central Alaska

The famous place is:

All the answers for your
Which Way adventure
are on the next two
pages. Do not go

unless you need help
with a puzzle. If you
don't need help,

before you look at
the answers.

You can use the rest of
this page to work out
your puzzles. If you need
a little extra space,

your pencil here. After
you're done, make a

back to the page you
were working on.

ANSWERS

Pages 2-3: Whale, Whale!

When unscrambled, the shaded letters spell BARTLETT. On page 28, cross off Edward Lewis Bartlett.

Pages 4-5: Face Facts

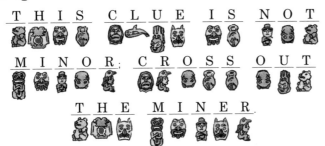

THIS CLUE IS NOT MINOR; CROSS OUT THE MINER.

On page 28, cross off Joseph Juneau.

Pages 6-7: On Ice

On page 28, cross off Carl Ben Eielson, the bush pilot.

Pages 8-9: Fancy Footwork
1. **i** 2. **d** 3. **i** 4. **t** 5. **a** 6. **r** 7. **o** 8. **d**
Eliminate the person associated with the IDITAROD. Cross off Susan Butcher on page 28.

Pages 10-11: Green Giants
Jack and Ava are correct. On page 28, you can cross off the painter, Howard Rock.

Pages 12-13: Piping Hot

1. $\underset{1}{A}$ N $\underset{2}{C}$ $\underset{}{H}$ O R $\underset{3}{A}$ G E

2. $\underset{}{E}$ X X $\underset{4}{O}$ N   V A L $\underset{5}{D}$ E Z

3. $\underset{6}{B}$ A R B A R A   W $\underset{7}{A}$ S H B U R $\underset{8}{N}$

4. $\underset{9}{A}$ $\underset{10}{L}$ E $\underset{11}{U}$ T I A N

5. $\underset{12}{K}$ I N G $\underset{13}{S}$ A L M $\underset{14}{O}$ N

On page 29, cross off

$\underset{1}{A}$ $\underset{9}{L}$ $\underset{9}{L}$ $\underset{11}{T}$ $\underset{2}{H}$ $\underset{10}{E}$ $\underset{7}{W}$ $\underset{4}{O}$ $\underset{8}{R}$ $\underset{5}{D}$ $\underset{13}{S}$ $\underset{11}{T}$ $\underset{2}{H}$ $\underset{1}{A}$ $\underset{11}{T}$

$\underset{6}{B}$ $\underset{10}{E}$ $\underset{3}{G}$ $\underset{12}{I}$ $\underset{14}{N}$ $\underset{7}{W}$ $\underset{12}{I}$ $\underset{11}{T}$ $\underset{2}{H}$ $\underset{13}{S}$ $\underset{1}{A}$ $\underset{14}{N}$ $\underset{5}{D}$ $\underset{11}{T}$.

Pages 14-15: Mush!

The clue for page 29 is: Cross off all the words with <u>6</u> letters.

Pages 16-17: Truly Spectacular
The entries about the pipeline, Sitka, and Anchorage are true. Since half the entries are true, the clue for page 29 is: Cross off the words with only four letters.